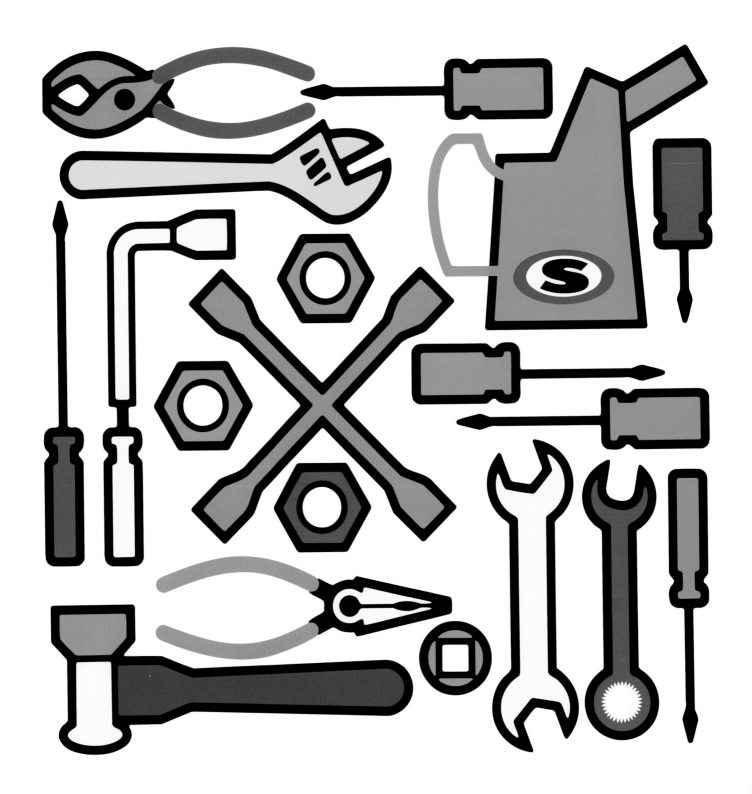

STANLEY'S GARAGE
A JONATHAN CAPE BOOK 978 1 780 08127 4
Published in Great Britain by Jonathan Cape,
an imprint of Random House Children's Publishers UK
A Penguin Random House Company

First published in hardback by Jonathan Cape in 2014
This edition published 2015

001

RANDOM HOUSE CHILDREN'S PUBLISHERS UK
61–63 Uxbridge Road, London W5 5SA
www.**randomhousechildrens**.co.uk
www.**randomhouse**.co.uk

Addresses for companies within The Random House Group Limited can be found at: www.randomhouse.co.uk/offices.htm
THE RANDOM HOUSE GROUP Limited Reg. No. 954009
A CIP catalogue record for this book is available from the British Library.
Printed in China

Penguin Random House is committed to a sustainable future for our business, our readers and our planet.
This book is made from Forest Stewardship Council® certified paper.

williambee
Stanley's
Garage

JONATHAN CAPE • LONDON

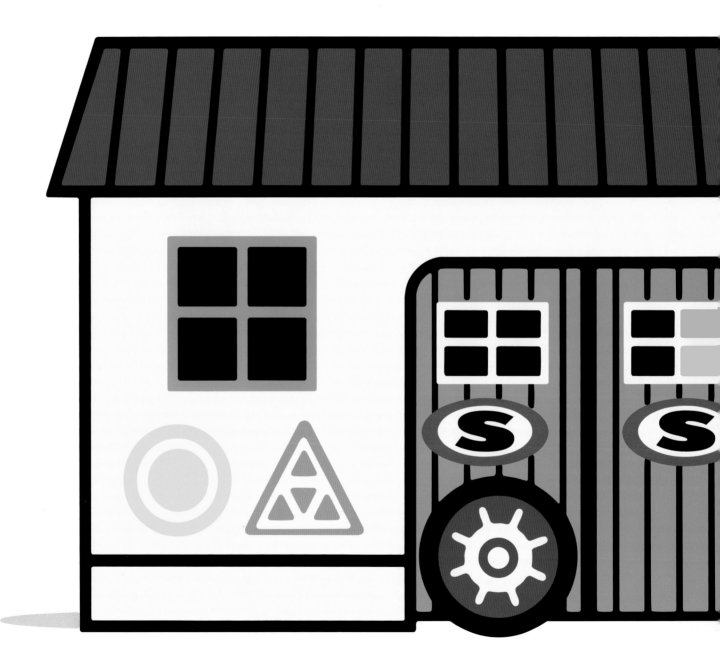

This is Stanley's garage.
Who will drive in today?

Here is Stanley's friend Hattie.

She needs some petrol for her
red sports car.

And here are Shamus and Little Woo.

Oh dear! Shamus's blue car has a flat tyre.

Stanley jacks the car up and changes the flat tyre for a nice round one.

Shamus and Little Woo say:
"Thank you, Stanley!"

Now what is causing all this smoke?

It's Charlie's yellow car. It's overheating.

Stanley quickly tops up the radiator
with cold water.

Ring! Ring! Ring! Ring!
Stanley's telephone is ringing.
It's Myrtle - her car has broken down
on the way to the shops.

Stanley drives out in his tow truck.

He tows Myrtle's purple car - and Myrtle -
back to the garage.

Stanley puts Myrtle's car up on the ramp.
Stanley gets very oily – but he soon
fixes the problem.

. . . And off Myrtle goes!
Thank you, Stanley!

Well! What a busy day!

Stanley's
House

Time for tea!
Time for a bath!

And time for bed!
Goodnight, Stanley.

Stanley

If you liked **Stanley's Garage** then you'll
love these other books about Stanley:

Stanley the Builder
Stanley the Farmer
Stanley's Café